D0922687

DATE DUE		
MY 10 13		
N 13 B		
FE 03 14		
N 01 14		
JAN 05 2015		
GAYLORD		PRINTED IN U.S.A.

Tales from Shakespeare

A Midsummer Night's Dream

Oberon — King of the fairies

Titania — Queen of the fairies

Puck — Oberon's servant

Hippolyta Queen of the Amazons

Hermia Engaged to Lysander

Helena In love with Demetrius

Theseus The duke of Athens

Egeus Hermia's father

Lysander In love with Hermia

Demetrius Thinks he's in love with Hermia

Nick Bottom A weaver, tricked by the fairies

Peter Quince A carpenter, he puts on a play

C. A. Plaisted

Illustrated by Yaniv Shimony

QEB Publishing

A royal wedding is planned
Act one

The people of Athens were in the mood for a party. Theseus, the duke of Athens, was getting married to Hippolyta, queen of the Amazons, in just a few days' time. The couple was busy organizing their wedding in Theseus's palace, when they were interrupted by visitors.

"Hello, Egeus," Theseus said. "What can I do for you?"

Egeus had arrived with his daughter, Hermia. He was looking angry and impatient.

"I need your help, Theseus," Egeus explained, pointing at Hermia. "As you know, I want Hermia to marry Demetrius. He's the perfect match for her. Such a charming young man—and he loves her!"

"Oh, please!" huffed Hermia. "He's just awful—and I don't love him!"

Theseus and Hippolyta looked at each other and raised their eyebrows. Why were they being bothered with this nonsense when they had better things to do?

"She says that she loves Lysander!" Egeus exclaimed. "Theseus! Tell her this will never do."

Theseus looked at Hermia. He didn't have time for her sulking.

"Young lady," Theseus said, irritably, "you know very well that Athenian law states that you should follow your father's wishes. If he says you are going to marry Demetrius, then you will."

"I will not!" Hermia screamed.

"Quiet!" ordered Theseus. "I'll give you until my wedding day to come to your senses. If you don't obey your father by then, I will have you punished!"

Hermia was furious. She went straight to Lysander to tell him what had happened.

"Listen to me, Hermia," he whispered.

"I have an idea! My aunt lives just outside of Athens. She'll understand how much we love each other."

The course of true love never did run smooth
—Lysander

"We can get married at
her house, where Athenian
law cannot stop us!"

"Oh, Lysander," Hermia
swooned. "How I love you!"

"And I love you, too,"
Lysander said, smiling.
"Meet me in the forest
tomorrow night."

Just then, Hermia's
friend Helena arrived
and saw them kissing.

"What are you
two up to?" Helena
asked. "Hermia, I
thought you'd
be with
Demetrius.
Your father
told me you
were getting
married!"

"Or so he thinks," Hermia sneered. "Shall we tell her, my love?"

Lysander nodded and told Helena their plan. They made her swear to keep it a secret.

"How can Hermia treat Demetrius this way?" Helena said, as the couple left to get ready to elope.

For several months, Helena had been in love with Demetrius herself.

But no matter how much she flirted with him, he only had eyes for Hermia. Perhaps, Helena thought, if she told Demetrius what Hermia and Lysander were up to, this might be her chance to win Demetrius's love!

Helena set off to find him.

Elsewhere in the palace grounds, a group of men was also meeting in secret. Among them were Peter Quince, a carpenter, a tinker named Tom Snout, and a weaver named Nick Bottom. They all worked for Theseus and were plotting a marvelous surprise for him—they were planning to put on a play!

"Here," said Peter Quince, "take your scripts. If we practice enough, we'll be ready to perform our play on the night of the wedding!"

Peter   Nick   Tom   Francis   Snug   Robin
Quince   Bottom   Snout   Flute   Starveling

Their play was
to be called "Pyramus
and Thisbe."
"We should
rehearse in the woods,"
Quince continued.
"Otherwise we'll never
keep this play a
surprise!"
And so the
men agreed to meet
in the woods that
night—the very
same moonlit woods
where Lysander
and Hermia also
planned to meet...

The fairies plot their magic

Act two

How could any of the poor fools have realized how busy the woods were going to be that night? Oberon, king of the fairies, had decided to hold a party in the palace woods to celebrate the royal wedding.

Ill met by moonlight, proud Titania

—*Oberon*

It wasn't long before Oberon began to argue with Titania, the fairy queen.

"You owe me a favor, Titania, and I know how to settle it," Oberon declared. "Let me have your servant boy. He can come and work for me."

9

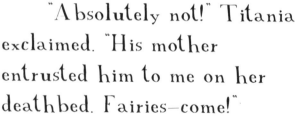

"Absolutely not!" Titania
exclaimed. "His mother
entrusted him to me on her
deathbed. Fairies—come!"

With her attendants
following behind her,
Titania flew away
in anger.

"How dare she
disappear like that!"
Oberon said, turning
to his loyal
hobgoblin,

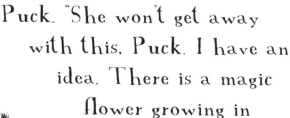

Puck. "She won't get away
with this, Puck. I have an
idea. There is a magic
flower growing in
these woods.

It's known as
love-in-
idleness,"
Oberon said.

"Find that flower, Puck, and bring it back to me. If I place a drop of its juice in Titania's sleeping eyes, I can enchant her and get the boy!"

"As you wish, sir," replied Puck. He winked and disappeared in a flash.

Oberon sat alone in the woods, plotting his revenge. But his thoughts were disturbed by the voices of Demetrius and Helena, who had entered the woods. Knowing that the humans would not be able to see him, Oberon decided to eavesdrop on the pair.

I love thee not, therefore pursue me not
—Demetrius

"I wish you would stop following me, Helena!" Demetrius said, sighing. "I've told you—I don't love you.

It's Hermia that I want. But where is she? You said that she was going to meet Lysander here and run away with him!"

Poor Helena. No matter how horrible Demetrius was to her, she still loved him. "But I love you, Demetrius!" Helena wailed.

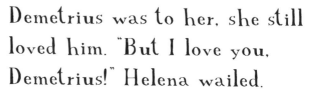
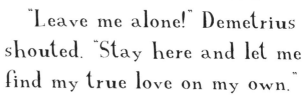

And I am sick when I look not on you
—Helena

"Leave me alone!" Demetrius shouted. "Stay here and let me find my true love on my own."

Helena watched as Demetrius fled. But a few minutes later, she set off to follow him again. Helena had no idea that Oberon had witnessed her humiliation.

"He'll change his mind," Oberon said, as Puck returned to him. "I'll make sure of that. You have the flower?"

Puck nodded.

"Excellent," Oberon said, taking the magical blossom with a grin. "Now, do as I say..."

Puck listened intently to his master.

"Take some of this flower juice in your hands. Follow the young lady who has just passed through here. She'll be running after a man."

Puck nodded.

"You'll recognize them because of their Athenian clothes. When you find the man, bewitch him with this juice. Just make sure that you get all of this done before dawn!"

"I'll do everything you say," Puck agreed, flying off.

Oberon set off to find Titania. He found her drifting off to sleep as she listened to her fairies making music. Creeping up alongside her, Oberon sprinkled the magical flower juice onto Titania's eyes.

"Ha!" Oberon said to himself.

What thou see'st when thou does wake, do it for thy true-love take
—Oberon

"When she wakes up, she'll fall in love with the first person she sees. I wonder how she'll like that!" Oberon snickered and left Titania to her slumber.

It didn't take Puck long to find the young couple that Oberon had told him about. They were resting by a stream and had both fallen asleep.

Here's a man in Athenian clothes, he thought to himself, as he hovered over the sleepy fellow. Puck would do just as Oberon said...

Plip, plop! The magical flower juice fell onto the man's eyes. As Puck flew off again, he had no idea that he had enchanted the wrong man. Instead of casting Oberon's spell on Demetrius, Puck had bewitched another man in Athenian clothes. The other man was Lysander, who was fleeing Athens with Hermia...

If only Puck had flown the other way across the woods, he would have found Demetrius racing along another path, desperate to escape from Helena.

Helena was exhausted and unable to keep up with Demetrius. She sat down by the stream to rest.

"I wish I was Hermia," Helena said, sighing. "She's not only beautiful, but she loves a man who loves her back..."

Helena stretched her arms and yawned. Then suddenly she spied a sleeping couple farther along the bank.

Helena raced over to the pair. Was it Lysander and Hermia? Were they hurt? They should have been far away by now...

"Thank goodness, there's no blood," Helena exclaimed, as she touched Lysander.

"Helena?" Lysander said, as he opened his eyes. "Is this beautiful creature I see before me Helena?"

Helena looked at Lysander in disbelief. What was he talking about? Had he gone crazy? "Are you joking? You're in love with Hermia! Why are you flirting with me?"

Lysander, enchanted by Oberon's spell, shook his head. "I got it wrong," he said. "Hermia's been driving me crazy. It isn't her I love. Helena—I love you!"

Helena stepped back in shock. Lysander grabbed her hand, kissing it. This was all wrong. She loved Demetrius, not Lysander. And Lysander loved Hermia!

"Stop mocking me!" Helena shrieked, pulling her hand away and running off. "Leave me alone!"

"But I love you!" Lysander called out, chasing after her.

Disturbed by all the commotion, Hermia woke up. Looking around, she realized she was on her own.

"Lysander? Where can he be? I must find him!"

Worried and afraid, Hermia set off to find her love.

Alone in her fairy bower, Titania was now the only one still asleep in the woods...

The woods are far from quiet...

Act three

On his way home, Puck came across Peter Quince and his friends. They were busy rehearsing their play.

"Well! I never!" Puck whispered. "I must see this—maybe I'll even join in!"

Puck watched as the men fumbled around, rehearsing their lines. But he was soon bored and wondered what tricks he could play to cause some mischief.

"That one is wandering off on his own," Puck whispered, following Nick Bottom into the bushes. "I'll play a trick on him and liven this bunch up a bit. He's as silly as a donkey, so why don't I make him one?"

And with a flick of his fingers, Puck planted an ass's head on top of Bottom's.

Poor Bottom had no idea what had happened. As he wandered back from the bushes to continue with the play, he came across Tom Snout.

"Bottom!" Snout exclaimed. "What happened to you?"

The others
gathered around
and screamed.
"He's turned
into an ass!"
Quince shouted.
Bottom's
terrified friends ran
away from him as
fast as their feet could
carry them.

"What are they clowning around for?"
mumbled Bottom, who still had no idea
what had happened to him. "I'd better sit
here and wait for them to come back.
And if I sing, they'll see that
they haven't frightened me!"
Still snoring in her
fairy bower, Titania's
dreams were
interrupted by
Bottom's songs.

Wiping the sleep from her eyes, Titania
stretched and sat up.

"Who is singing so sweetly?" Titania
said to herself, unaware that Oberon had
enchanted her.

Titania found
Bottom, softly
humming his songs.

"You are the
most handsome
man I have ever
met!" Titania
cried, swooning at
Bottom's feet.

"Me?" Bottom
turned around to see
who else was there. There was
no one else around.

"Yes, you!" Titania
replied. "Come with me to my
bower. My fairies will wait
on you."

I pray thee, gentle
mortal, sing again.
Mine ear is much
enamored of
thy note
—Titania

23

Bottom had never seen such a beautiful creature in his entire life. And he'd certainly never spoken to one. So if Titania really did that think he was handsome, he was not going to argue.

"Well, then," Bottom said, grinning. "I guess I'd better come with you."

So Titania and her attendants led Bottom toward the fairy bower.

Puck couldn't wait to tell Oberon all of this. He found his master on the other side of the woods.

"This couldn't have turned out better!" Oberon cried.

He burst out laughing after
Puck had finished his story.
"Titania is in love with an
ass-headed man! But what
about the Athenian?"

"All fixed too, sir," Puck said, beaming.

Just then, Demetrius and Hermia
appeared among the trees. Either by luck
or by coincidence, their paths had crossed.
Oberon pulled Puck close to him.

"Well, there's the young
Athenian we were talking
about!" Oberon said.

Puck was puzzled. "It's
the young lady, yes. But it
isn't the same man, sir."

But Oberon didn't get
the chance to reply. Like
Puck, he was too busy
listening to Demetrius
and Hermia.

25

"Have you hurt Lysander?" Hermia asked Demetrius. He had found her while she was looking for Lysander in the woods. "Where have you hidden him?"

"I haven't touched him!" Demetrius protested. "And I have no idea where he is."

"I hate you!" Hermia screamed. "I can't even bear to be with you anymore."

Turning on her heels, Hermia fled from the woods.

It seems that there's nothing I can do to change her mind, Demetrius thought, slumping down on the ground. She would never love him now...Tired of so much arguing, Demetrius decided to rest his eyes.

Still in their hiding place, Oberon turned to Puck. "Now we have the chance to fix your mistake," he hissed to his hobgoblin. "Go and find Helena. Bring her here!"

Eager to please his master, Puck quickly flew off.

Oberon gently squeezed the last of the magic flower potion onto Demetrius's eyes.

"Sir!" Puck hissed. "I've found her— and the young man I got confused about. They're here!"

Oberon and Puck stepped back and watched as Helena appeared. She was being chased by Lysander.

"Why do you think I'm teasing you?" Lysander asked. "I love you!"

"Has Hermia put you up to this?" Helena demanded to know. "Why are you all making fun of me?"

Disturbed by their argument, Demetrius woke up. As soon as he opened his eyes, he saw Helena.

"Oh, beautiful Helena!" he called
out. "How perfect you are! May I kiss
you, please?"

"Demetrius?" Helena asked. She
couldn't believe what he had just said. The
man who had once shouted that he didn't
love her was now telling her that he did!

"Has everyone gone crazy this evening?"
Helena wailed. "Why are you all
mocking me?"

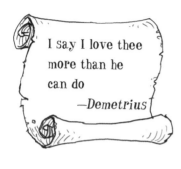

I say I love thee more than he can do
—Demetrius

But before Helena could figure out what was really going on, Hermia appeared.

"Lysander!" Hermia cried. "I've looked for you everywhere. You left me on my own!"

"Why should I stay with you when it is Helena that I love?" Lysander asked.

"You can't possibly love Helena as much as I do!" Demetrius protested.

"I'll fight a duel with you," Lysander said. "Then we'll see who loves Helena the most."

Demetrius followed Lysander to a clearing, ready to fight.

Now it was Hermia who couldn't believe what she was hearing. She glared at Helena.

"I thought you were my friend!" Hermia said. "How could you do this to me? Why have you tricked everyone?"

I pray you, though you mock me, gentlemen, let her not hurt me
—Helena

"Me?" Helena said. "You think I have tricked people? It's me that has been tricked. I wish you'd all leave me alone!" Helena turned and walked away.

Hermia stood alone in the woods, amazed.

From his hiding place, Oberon gave Puck an angry look.

"This is all your fault!" Oberon hissed. "If you hadn't gotten the wrong man in the first place, none of this would have happened."

Puck hung his head in shame.

"Go after those men!"
Oberon demanded. "Stop them
from fighting. But take this
herb with you. Make sure that
you crush it into Lysander's eyes.
With any luck, it will make
him think that all this has been a dream."

Puck nodded and flew off.

"I will go back to my Titania," Oberon
said to himself. "I've watched these humans
argue for long enough."

It was easy for
Puck to find
Demetrius and
Lysander. They
were fumbling
around in the
darkness, too tired
and confused to
fight this late
at night.

So when they had both given up any
attempt to duel, they each found a mossy
mound to rest on, then lay down and
fell asleep.

But before Puck could carry out
Oberon's wishes, Helena walked by.

The poor thing was exhausted from
everything that had happened and yawned.
It would take until morning to walk back
to Athens.

She sat down to rest her tired legs and
yawned again. Her eyes were so heavy, she
couldn't keep them open. Helena
started snoring gently as she
drifted off to sleep.

"And here
comes the other
lady!" Puck said to
himself, as Hermia
wandered past
him. She, too, felt
weary and sad.

She lay down and rested her head. She would stay here until morning.

Finally, they are all sleeping soundly, Puck thought.

Determined to make amends for his earlier mistake, Puck went over to Lysander and crushed the herb that his master had given him into the Athenian's eyes.

Soon they would all wake up and everything would be right again, Puck thought.

In your waking shall be shown. Jack shall have Jill, nought shall go ill, the man shall have his mare again, and all shall be well

—Puck

The spells are broken
Act four

Still wearing his ass's head, Bottom was relaxing in Titania's fairy bower. He was being waited on by the queen and her attendants, and he was loving every moment of their attention.

"Sweet man," Titania cooed into Bottom's ear, "what else can we do for you?"

Bottom thought for a moment and then yawned. "I'm feeling rather sleepy," Bottom said. "I'll just lie down here for a rest."

"Of course, my sweet," Titania replied. "Let me wrap my arms around you to keep you warm."

But just as the enchanted pair fell asleep, Oberon and Puck arrived.

Oberon smiled when he saw them. "She's so bewitched, I almost feel sorry for her."

Puck grinned.

"But this silliness has gone on for too long," Oberon said. "It's time that everything in Athens got back to normal. Puck, take off the ass's head. I will crush this herb into Titania's eyes to break the spell."

With their jobs done, Oberon gently woke his queen.

See'st thou this sweet sight? Her dotage now I do begin to pity...
—*Oberon*

"Oberon?" Titania said, rubbing her eyes. "You have no idea of the strange dreams I've had! I thought I was in love with an ass!"

"That's the man you were in love with," Oberon said, pointing to sleeping Bottom.

Titania shuddered at the sight of him. "Oberon, it's you I love."

"And I love you," Oberon replied. "Come with me, my queen. And let's not fight again."

And with Puck behind them, the fairy rulers flew away, leaving poor Bottom fast asleep.

As the sun rose in the morning sky, Theseus and Hippolyta arrived in the woods with Egeus. They were setting off on a morning's hunt to celebrate their wedding that evening. Riding around the woods, they came across Helena, Hermia, Demetrius, and Lysander. They were all still asleep, scattered under the trees.

"What's all this?" asked Theseus. He turned to Egeus. "Isn't it today that Hermia has to make up her mind?"

Egeus nodded, and Theseus summoned a huntsman to sound his horn to wake the four young people.

"It's about time you all got up!" Theseus called.

One by one, Hermia, Lysander, Helena, and Demetrius opened their eyes and rose.

> Fair lovers, you are fortunately met
> —*Theseus*

"I'm not sure how I got here," Lysander said, "but I think I was with Hermia, trying to run away from Athens."

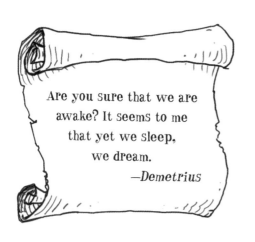

Are you sure that we are awake? It seems to me that yet we sleep, we dream.
—Demetrius

"Helena told me you were running away," Demetrius explained. "And I thought that I loved Hermia..." Demetrius looked at Helena. "But then I realized that it was Helena I really love," he said, taking her hand.

Theseus looked at Lysander and Hermia, then Helena and Demetrius. Then he looked at Egeus.

"I know this is not what you wanted, Egeus," Theseus said, "but these couples have made up their minds about who they love."

Egeus nodded and smiled at his daughter.

"Let them marry," he agreed.

"Indeed," said Theseus, taking his own bride's hand. "Come on—I think we've found what we were hunting for. Let's get back to Athens. I want to get married!"

> Methought I was—and methought I had—but man is but a patched fool if he will offer to say what methought I had
> —Bottom

In his bower, now deserted by the fairies, Bottom stirred. Had he been dreaming? He scratched his face. It was no longer hairy. He was sure that it had been.

He touched his ears. They weren't long... Bottom was sure that he remembered a beautiful girl. She'd kissed him!

But Bottom shook his head. No. It must have been nothing more than a dream. "Oh well," he said to himself, "I'd better get back to my friends. We have a play to perform!"

Bottom found his friends back at Peter Quince's house.

"We've been waiting for you!" Quince exclaimed, patting his friend on the back. "The play is hopeless without you."

Bottom smiled. "Well, I'm here now. Come on—let's go to the palace!"

The celebrations begin

Act five

Athens had never seen such a party! Theseus and Hippolyta had made plans for the most extravagant wedding. All of Athens turned out to cheer the royal couple. Everyone wished them happiness, as they knew how much the pair were in love.

Theseus and Hippolyta were so happy to be married at last that they invited Lysander and Hermia, and Demetrius and Helena, to celebrate their own weddings with them that day, too. Even Egeus was pleased to see his daughter so happy.

With all three wedding ceremonies over, everyone gathered at Theseus's palace for the wedding feast.

Here come the lovers, full of joy and mirth
—*Theseus*

As they gorged on their last drops of food and drink, Theseus clapped his hands together.

"So," he said. "Who is going to entertain us?"

Peter Quince bravely stepped forward. "Sir," he said, bowing, "we—that's me and my friends who all work for you—we have been practicing a play for you!"

Theseus smiled. "Excellent," he said. "Then you can perform it now!"

Bottom and his friends acted their hearts out. Their audience was captivated by the simplicity of their words, their humorous acting, and their sincerity. Once the play was over, the audience stood up to applaud. Bottom and his friends were overjoyed.

"Shall we do some more, sir?" Bottom asked, enjoying the attention.

Theseus shook his head.

"No," he said. "I think we should all dance now. After all, it will soon be time for bed."

So the Athenians danced until the clock struck midnight, when Theseus clapped his hands together again. "Time we should all be in our beds. It's almost fairy time! Good night, everyone."

One by one, the guests went home. Demetrius with his new wife, Helena. Lysander with his Hermia. Soon, every Athenian had rested his or her head on a pillow.

And, high above the earthly world, Oberon and Titania looked down upon the mortals.

"Let them have a shimmering of fairy light as they sleep," Oberon said, waving his hand.

"We should sing
and bless them all with
our fairy music," Titania
said, waving her hand.
A fairy chorus sang
sweetly, as their king
and queen
made their
way back
to their
bower.

If we shadows have
offended, think
but this, and all is
mended
—Puck

Lingering
behind, Puck looked at
Athens one final time.
"At last
everything is as
it should be," he
said. "Good night
to you all!"

The end

Consultant: Dr. Tamsin Theresa Badcoe
Editor: Alexandra Koken
Designer: Andrew Crowson

Copyright © QEB Publishing 2012

First published in the United States by
QEB Publishing, Inc
3 Wrigley, Suite A
Irvine, CA 92618

www.qed-publishing.co.uk

A CIP record for this book is available from the Library of Congress.

ISBN 978 1 60992 237 5

Printed in China